Crumple this
page

That's your last mistake.
Now smooth it out and
write what you learned on
the next page

→

What I Learned About Mistakes:

How did it feel to crumple the paper?

How did it feel to smooth out the paper?

Scribble out your fears in
the biggest, boldest lines
you can make.

Draw your "game face" as a superhero. Label its secret powers.

WRITE IT OUT

Write down 3 negative thoughts.

Now rip this page in half.

Make a victory pose collage using
cutouts, stickers, or drawings.

Create a Grit Meter.
Color it in based on today's
effort, not outcome.

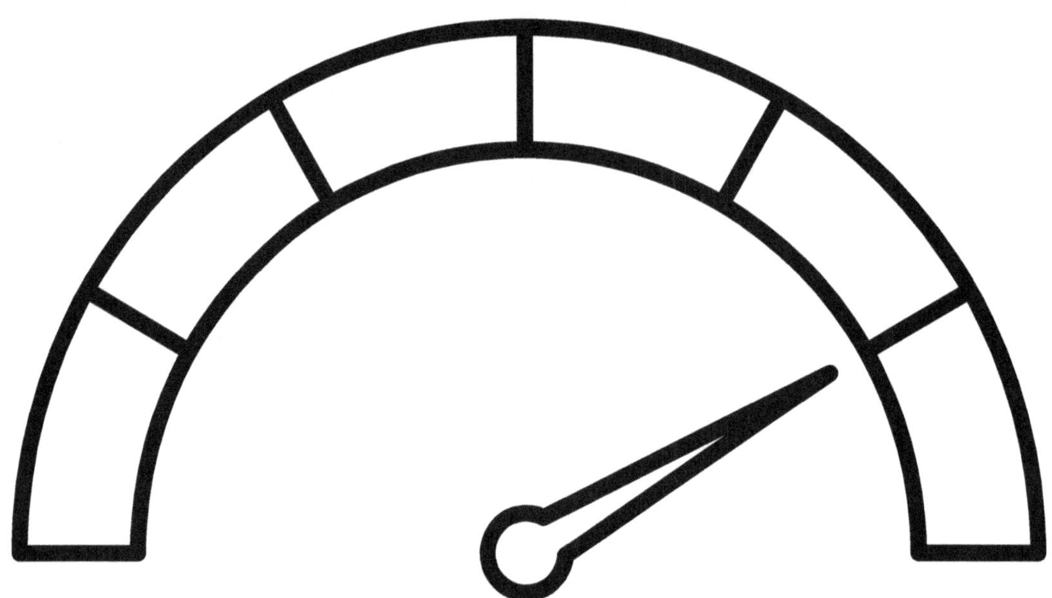

WRITE A PEP TALK TO
YOUR PAST SELF AFTER
A TOUGH GAME.

Draw your worst sports moment.
Then turn it into a comic strip.

List 10 thing's you've gotten better at. Star the one that took the most work

Stomp on this page.
That's what we do with self-doubt

Write your own trophy name. What do you win it for?

Create a playlist of your best mindset moments. What's the soundtrack?

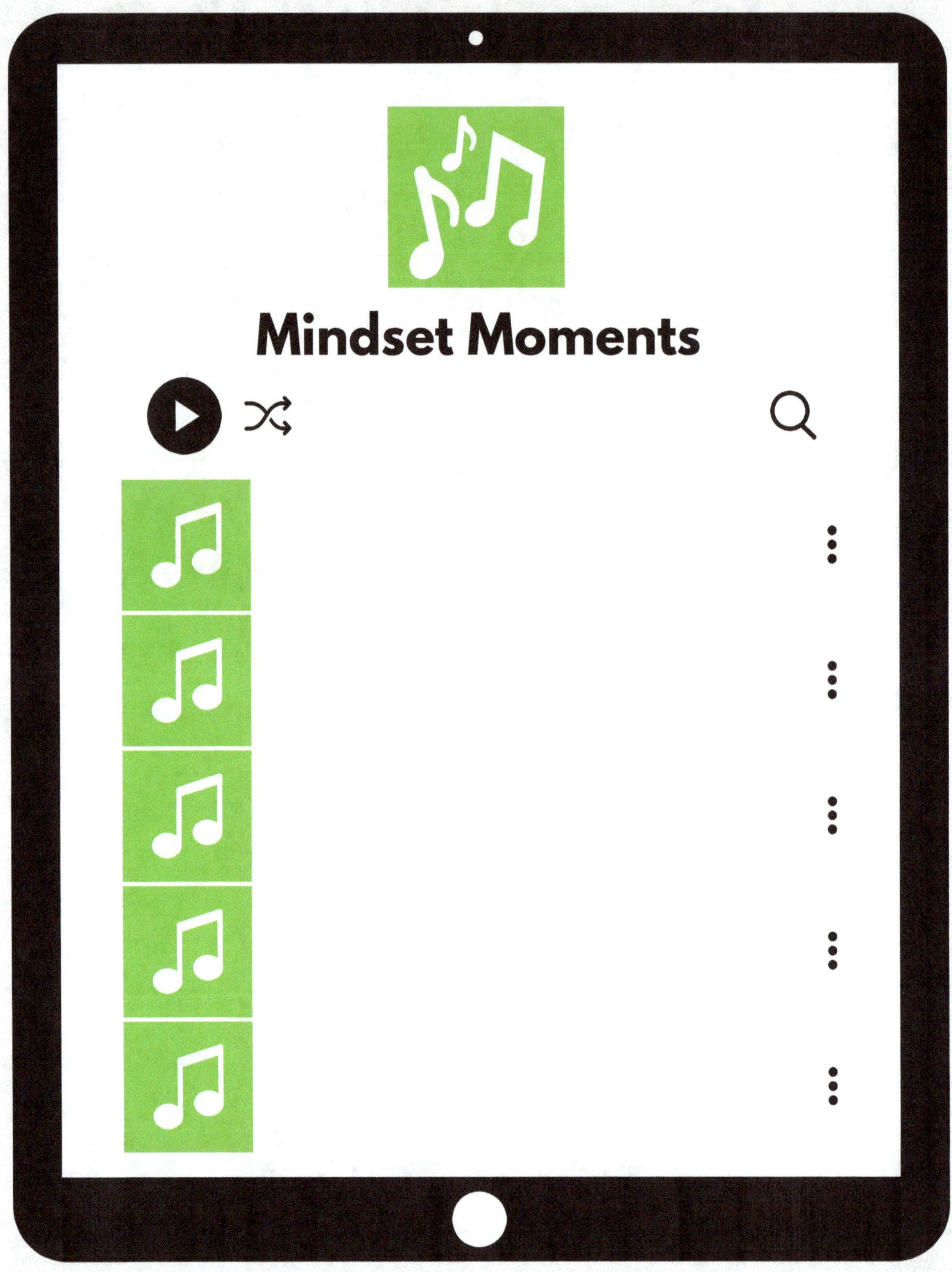

Fold this page into a paper ball
and shoot it like a free throw.

Confidence = RESET!

Tape in something from practice or a game. Label the lesson you learned.

Write with your non-dominant hand:
"I can do hard things."

Design your own team jersey with your personal motto.

Circle your proudest moment.
Then draw fireworks around it.

Write a secret wish for your future
in sports. Fold it into an envelope

Draw your mindset monster. What does it whisper? What shuts it up?

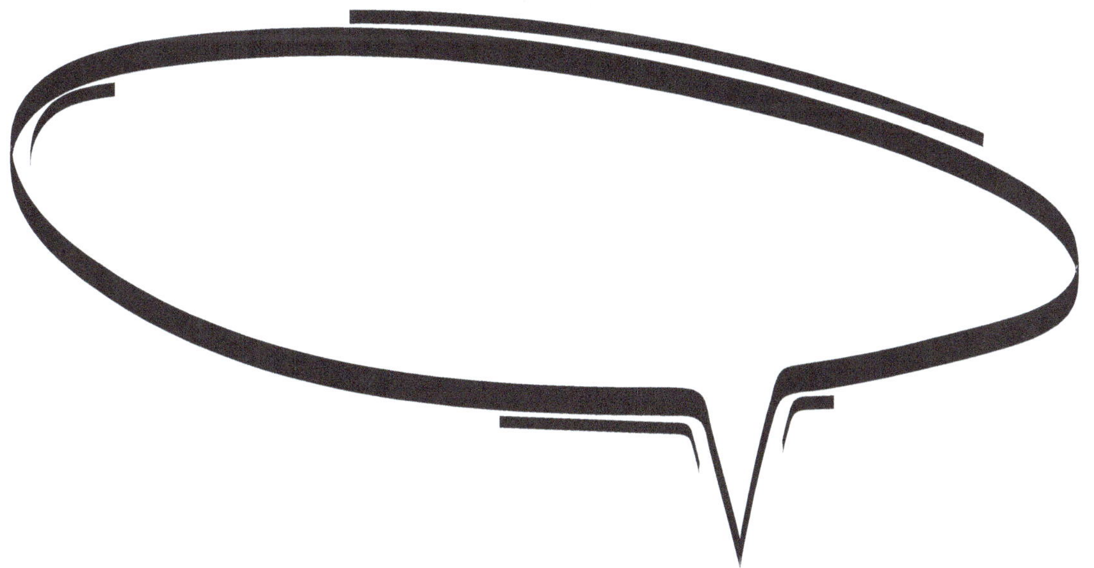

Write your own definition of success. No trophies allowed.

success
[səkˈses]

Give 3 examples of when you were successful

1.

2.

3.

**Tear this page.
Every rip is a barrier
breaking.**

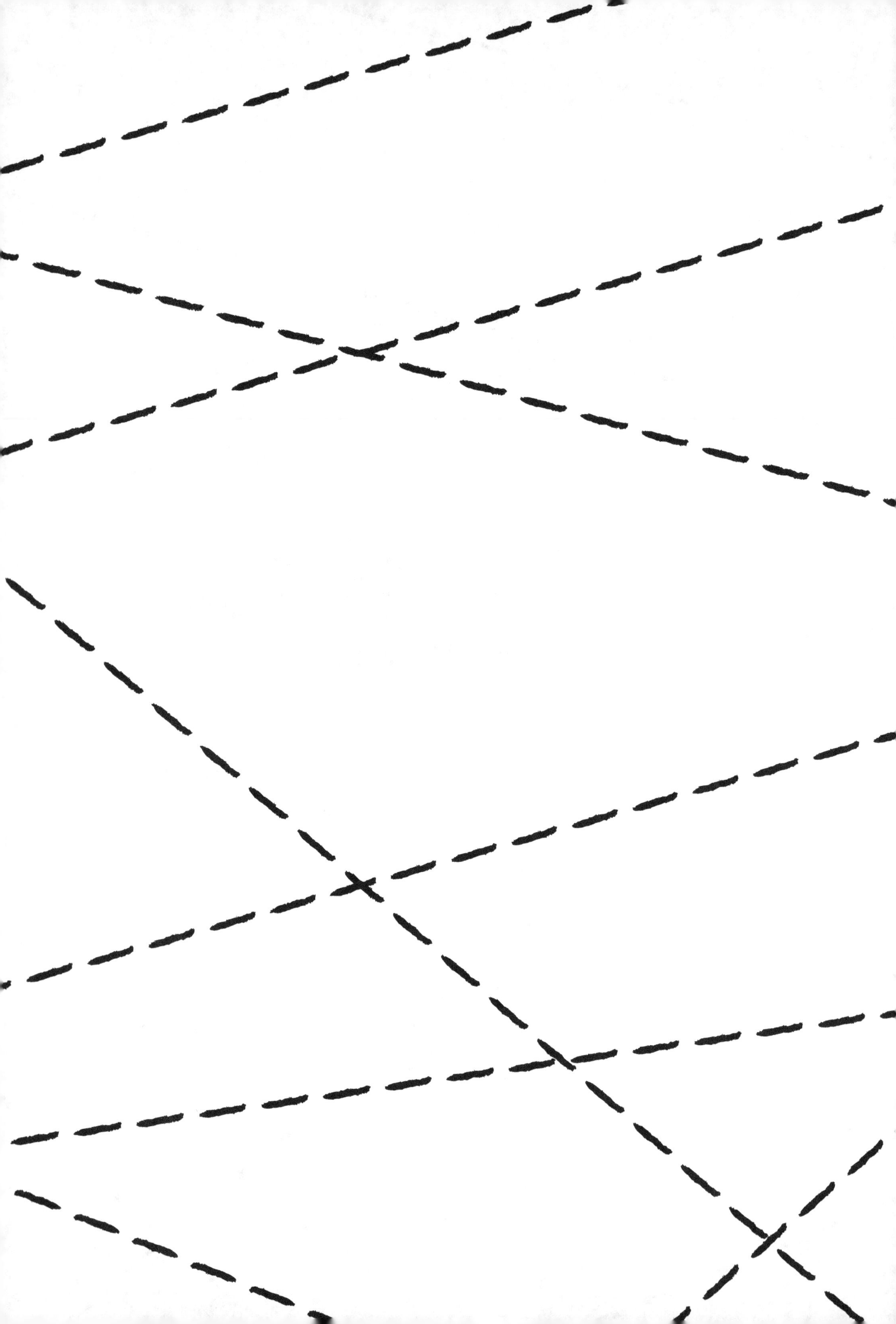

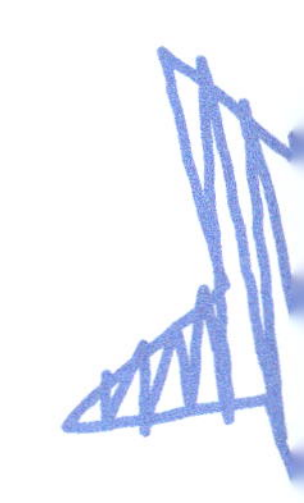

Write your pre-game nerves down.
Then black them out with a marker.

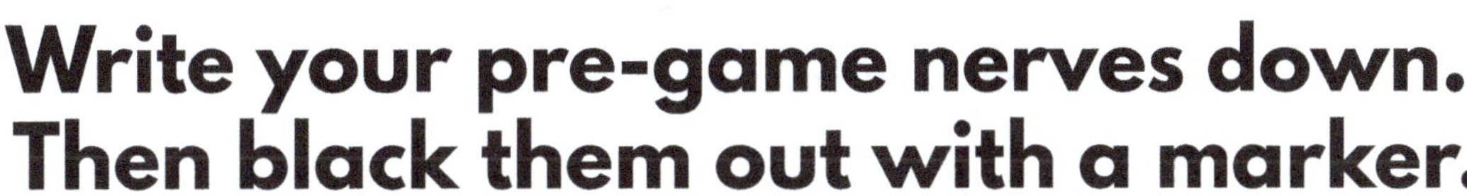

What am I most worried about today?

What are my physical sensations?

What negative thoughts are running through my head?

List 5 moments you wanted to quit—but didn't.

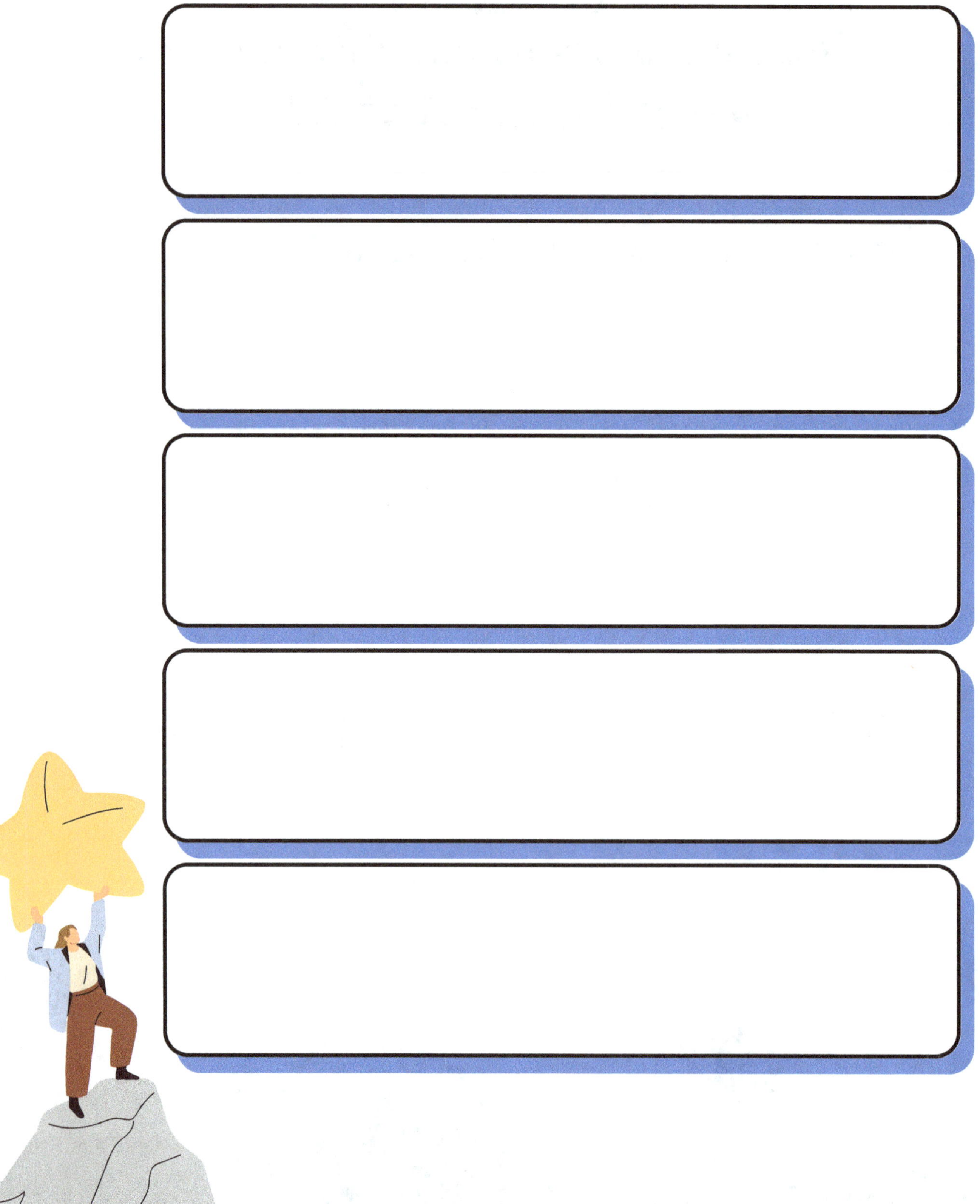

Create a "calm plan" for the next time you feel overwhelmed.

Draw a line for every practice this month.

Colour in the hard ones.

CONTRACT

DATE:

Dear Future Me,

Authorized Signature

Present Me

Stick something that smells like sports (tape, grass, sweatband)–and explain what it means to you.

make a doodle explosion
of everything that **PUMPS**
you up

Design your "comeback badge."
You earn it by getting up.

Write down words that make you strong
and words that don't.

Circle the strong words.

Cross out the weak words.

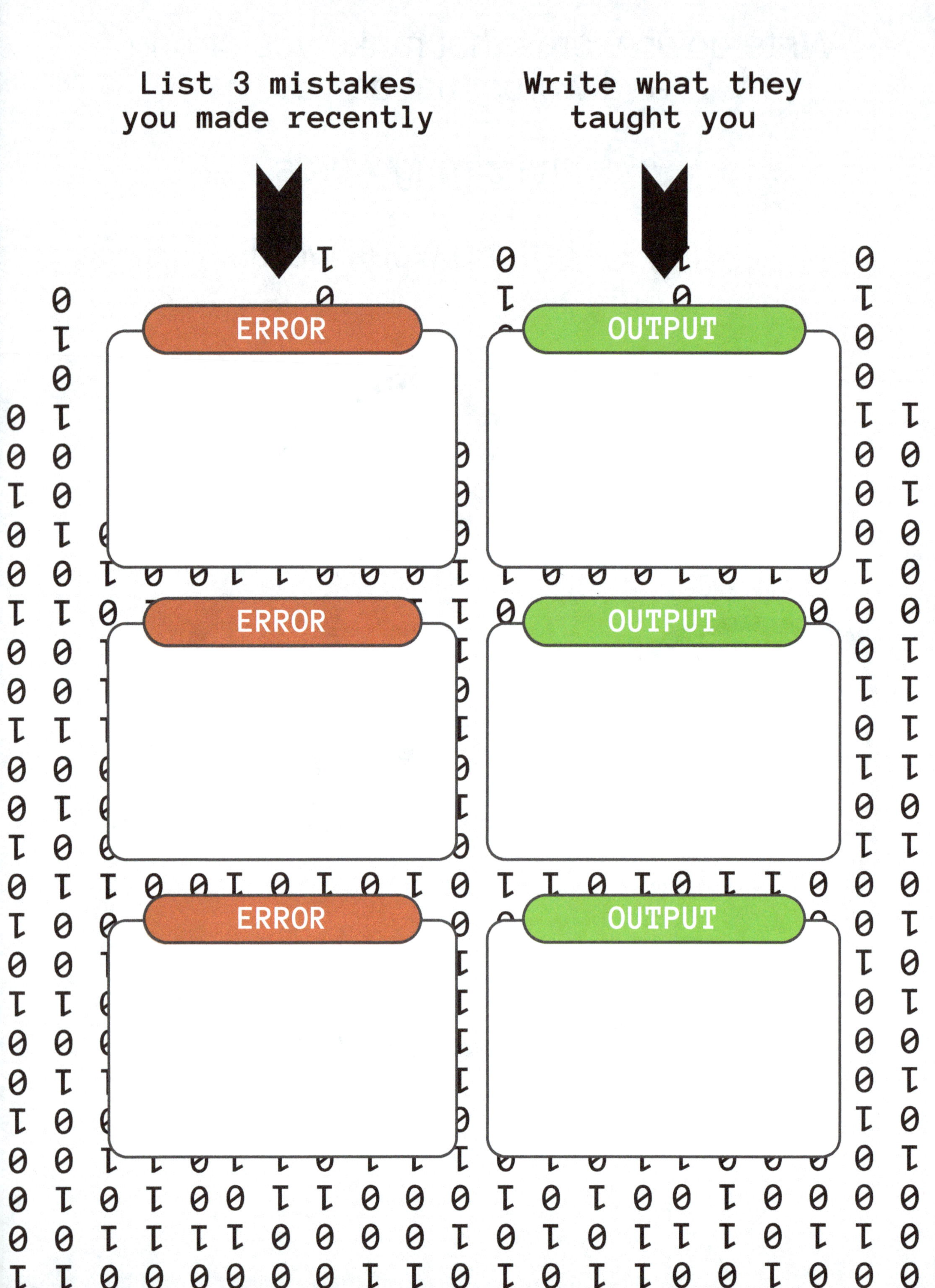

List 3 mistakes
you made recently

Write what they
taught you

ERROR

OUTPUT

ERROR

OUTPUT

ERROR

OUTPUT

Draw your sport using only shapes. It doesn't have to be perfect —just like effort.

Create a
"COACH IN YOUR HEAD"

What do they say when things get hard?

Draw your comfort zone.
Then step outside of it - literally.

Write a letter to a teammate who inspires you

To the legendary ________________

Cheers,

TRAINING COMPONENT	EXERCISE	VARIABLE

Design your own drill that trains both your brain and body.

WHY IM DUMPING YOU

Make a timeline of your growth
from nervous rookie to now.

TO BE CONTINUED

WRITE YOUR NAME LIKE A CHAMPIONSHIP BANNER. DECORATE IT WITH YOUR VALUES.

Create a "mental warm-up" routine. List it like game-day prep.

MENTAL WARM UP

1.

2.

3.

4.

5.

draw your

BIGGEST FAILURE

on this side of
the page

on the other side, draw

what came from it

WRITE 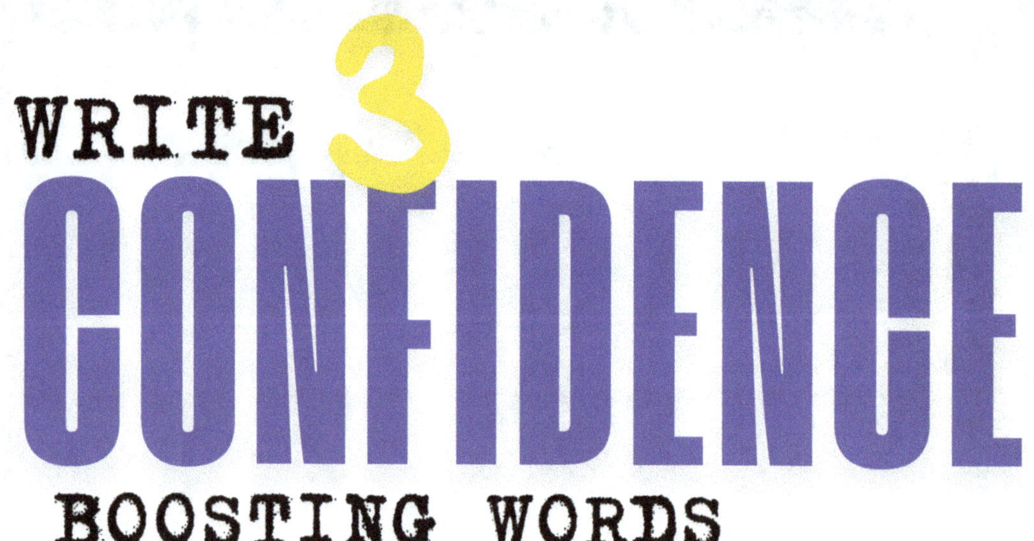

WRITE **3**
CONFIDENCE
BOOSTING WORDS

____

____

FILL THE WHOLE PAGE WITH THEM!

DESIGN A PRESSURE MONSTER

Glue, tape, or draw your biggest win

Explain what made
it special:

Write what you'd tell a younger athlete struggling with self-doubt.

COVER THIS PAGE IN
COLOUR

THE LOUDER. THE
BETTER

CONFIDENCE
IS LOUD!

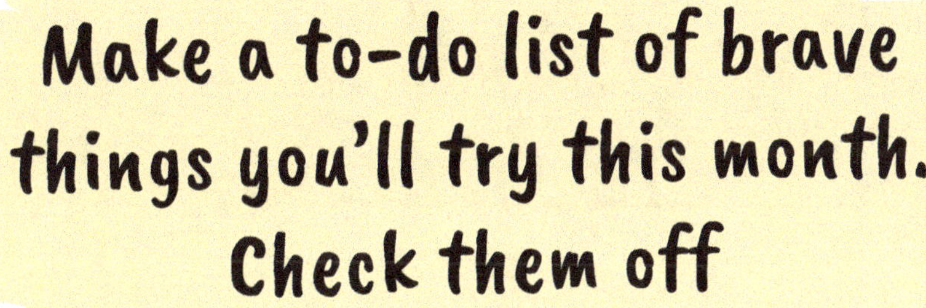

Make a to-do list of brave
things you'll try this month.
Check them off

write a page of
TRASH TALK
you'd NEVER say
to yourself

then destroy it.

**Draw your progress like a mountain.
Label the tough parts.**

Make a fear jar. Write down fears and "lock" them inside with tape.

Leave a page for your future self.
What do you hope they remember?

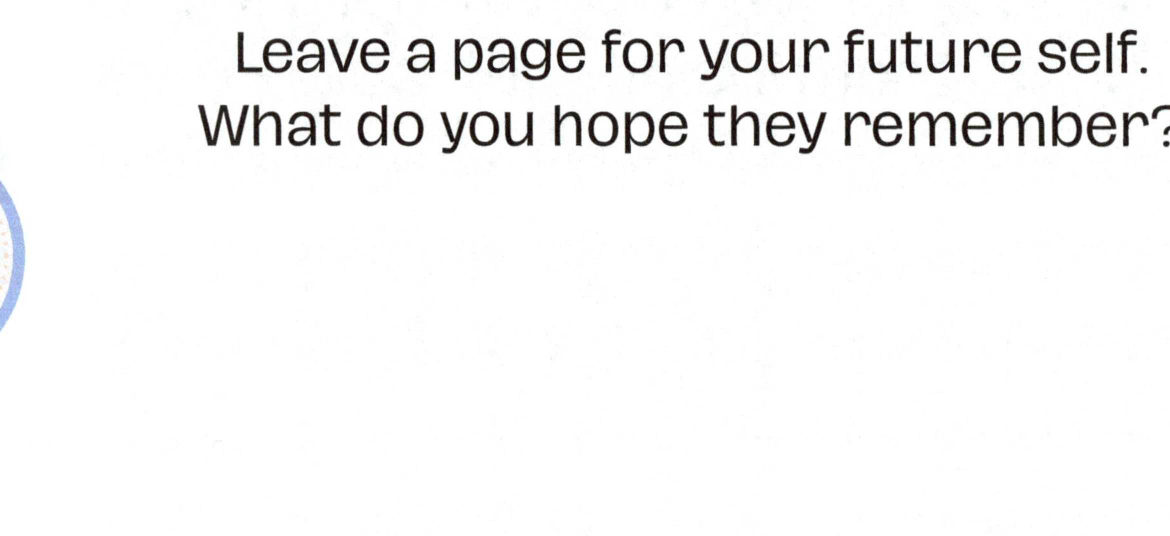

Create a collage of 3 things you're grateful for

Cover the page with your
positive affirmations

DRAW TWO VERSIONS OF YOURSELF

One representing your current athletic self

The other representing your ideal athletic self

What are the key differences?

LIST 5 SKILLS YOU WANT TO MASTER

CROSS THEM OFF AS YOU ACHIEVE THEM

01

02

03

04

05

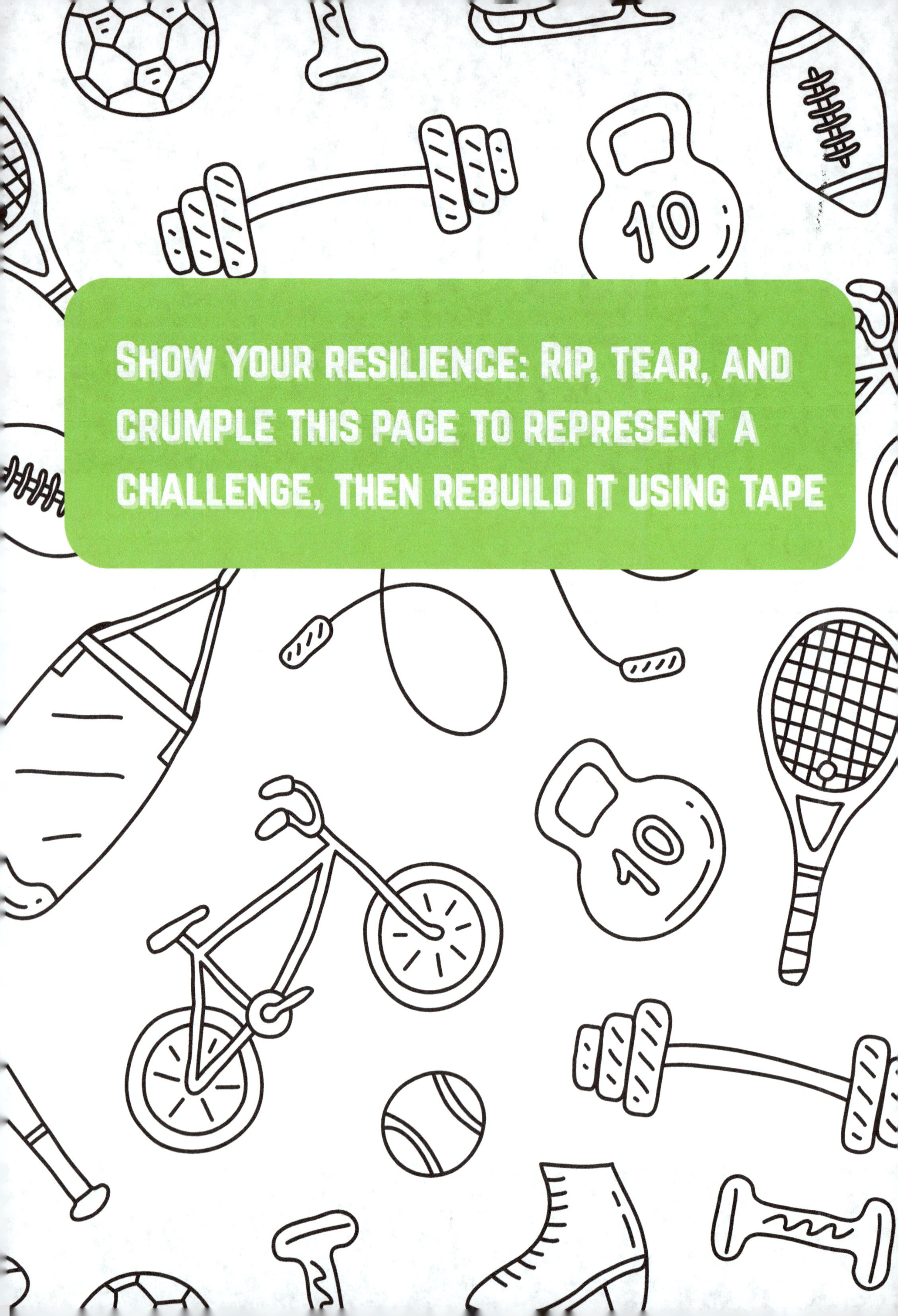

Show your resilience: Rip, tear, and crumple this page to represent a challenge, then rebuild it using tape

WRITE POSITIVE
FEEDBACK RECEIVED

THEN HIGHLIGHT IT WITH BRIGHT COLOURS

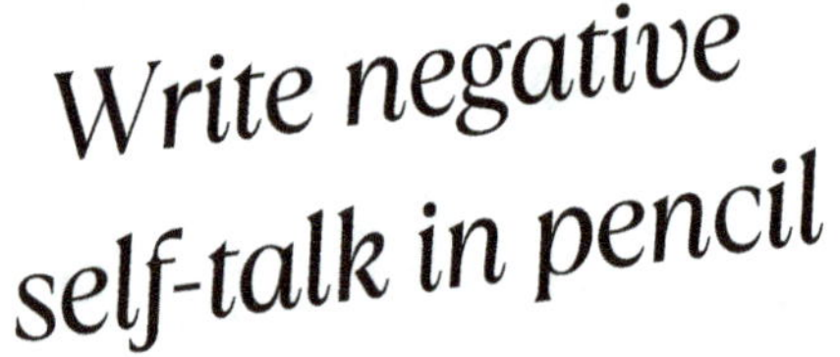
Write negative
self-talk in pencil

Then cover it with positive
affirmations in red pen

DRAW A BRAIN AND LABEL AREAS YOU WANT TO IMPROVE FOCUS IN

CUT OUT OR DRAW PICTURES OF
healthy foods
AND CREATE A COLLAGE OF YOUR IDEAL MEAL PLAN

Design a futuristic hydration device that tracks your water intake and reminds you to drink.

Draw the device and explain how it works

PAGE 2

Design a futuristic hydration device that tracks your water intake and reminds you to drink.

Draw the device and explain how it works

DESIGN A

BINGO

CARD

EACH SQUARE CONTAINS A DIFFERENT RECOVERY METHOD

CHECK OFF THE SQUARES AS YOU COMPLETE THEM THROUGHOUT THE WEEK

BINGO

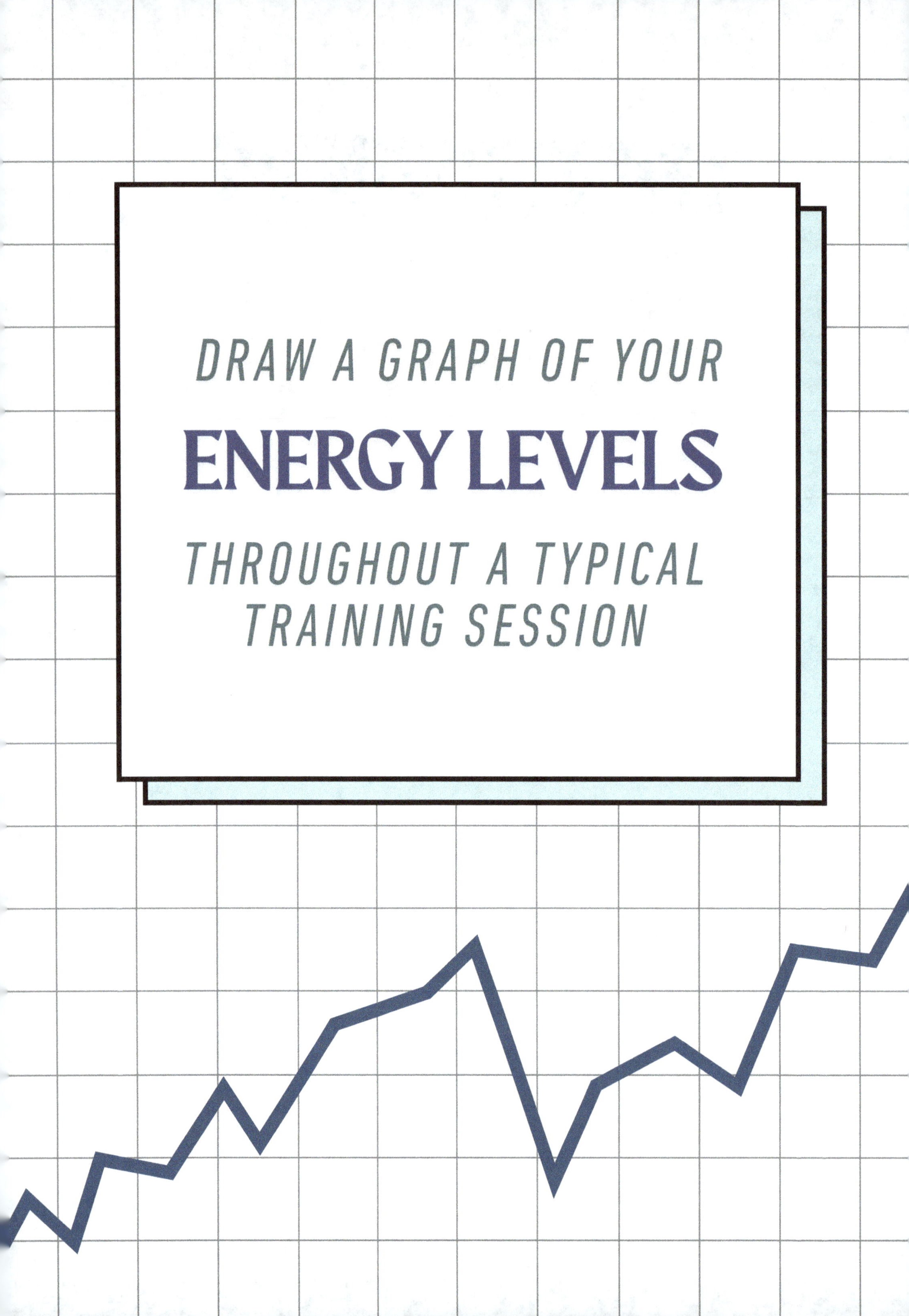

DRAW A GRAPH OF YOUR
ENERGY LEVELS
THROUGHOUT A TYPICAL
TRAINING SESSION